AF265765

"Oh My!.......
I Wonder Why"

Bella's Story

Paperback ISBN: 978-1-971650-86-9

Dedicated to:

The memory of my dear friend Janice Ann Carey, whose laughter was a gift, whose friendship shaped my heart and whose spirit continues to walk with me through the halls of time. For every moment we shared and every dream we held close, may you now know the fullness of God's love. Rest, my friend until we meet again.

Opening Page:

Free indeed, Barry bird continued to soar above the mountains.
He crossed over the rivers and swooped low in the valleys. With his newfound freedom, he looked
forward to the adventures which lay ahead.
"What would he find?"
"Who would he meet?"
Only Time Will Tell… Time Will Tell

Barry's flight brought him to a
bustling little town. The sign read, "Agape
Meadow Park; All are
welcome".
Drawn by the laughter of children,
rustling leaves, and green trees, Barry
thought "This looks like a good place to
rest after my long flight."

Agape Meadow Park
All Are Welcome

As he perched on a sturdy oak branch. He looked out and noticed a small blue bird sitting alone in the next tree.

"Hello!" he cried out. "My name is Barry, what's yours?"
Bella! But it's none of your business. This is my park. You don't belong here was her reply.

Barry sat shocked! Oh my…. I wonder why? Bella is so mean, he thought. Barry could hear the rumors being whispered in the trees.
Bella was small and not very pretty, they said. She was too loud, too fast, and the most mischievous blue jay around. Bella was disliked by everyone.

Bella had a problem. She was a bully, and no one liked her at all.
The other animals in Agape Meadow Park tried hard to stay away whenever she was around.
Bella enjoyed being mean.

Every afternoon, while the
children gathered in the park to play,
Bella made sure she always popped their
colored balloons.
She especially loved to hear the loud pop
and see the children cry. She swooped
down and pulled their kites out of the air
just for fun.

POP!
HA
HA HA
!

"Oh my.... I wonder why,"
Barry thought. He tilted his head towards
Bella and asked, "Does causing others
sadness truly make you happy Bella?"

"It's just fun," Bella replied. "I can do what
I want; this is my park, and you can't stop
me."

As the days went by, Barry watched Bella's antics. He watched her fly low so she could scare the little sparrows.
He noticed when she stole food from the picnickers and couldn't believe it when she hid the acorns, so the squirrels went hungry.
It made Barry sad when she pecked at the ducks in the pond, laughing as she flew away. "Oh my…. This isn't kind at all," Barry said.

Barry wondered, "Doesn't Bella ever get lonely." He looked around the park. The squirrels played together, the sparrows chirped happily in a little group, and even the ducks paddled side by side. But Bella was always alone.

Bella's antics troubled Barry.
He knew beneath her mischievous ways lay
a heart capable of kindness and care.
He was determined to help Bella learn the
lessons of love.

Early the next morning, the clouds started turning dark. Everyone scurried out of the park, running as fast as they could.
"Oh my.... I wonder why?"
Barry never could have imagined what was coming next.

NATURE
RESERVE

Strong winds and rain began to blow
through the park, soaking the ground and
shaking the trees.
Bella's nest wobbled, tumbled, and fell to
the wet ground. Her home was shattered,
twigs and leaves were flying everywhere.

"Oh No!" Bella gasped. "The wind is carrying my home away."
She tried to catch the leaves & twigs, but the wind was too fierce.
Bella was now in trouble. What could she do?

Barry watched Bella struggle.
He turned to the other animals
huddling close together and said, "Bella
needs our help! Let's all work
together and show her how much we care."

Let's help Bella

"No way!" Cried Sammy the squirrel.
"Why should we help her" Stella the Sparrow chimed in.
"Let her do it herself," said Charlie the chipmunk.
"This is what she gets for being so nasty."

Barry spoke up, "Maybe all she needs is a friend," He announced.
"Sometimes, when you are hurting on the inside, you hurt others on the outside," Barry explained.
Love is kind, and love is patient. If we can all forgive her, perhaps Bella can change.
"Loving our enemies and doing good when they hurt us is hard, but we could try," Barry suggested.

The park animals began to whisper among themselves. They nodded to each other.
"Barry's right," Charlie cried.
Slowly, one by one, working together, they picked up fresh twigs & leaves and began to help rebuild Bella's nest.

Bella watched from a distance. "What are they doing?" She wondered.
Expecting to feel mean and angry....
She didn't, not this time. Bella felt something strange; it fluttered her heart. What was happening? She was feeling so grateful and happy.

"Oh! My...I wonder why?" She asked Barry.

"You see Bella, love has a way of changing us. We're your friends; a true friend loves at all times, even when you're not kind," Barry told her.

Bella had never noticed Barry's
radiant feathers until now. Hers looked
nothing like that.
"How can I change?"
Bella whispered to Barry.

"By choosing love over mischief," Barry
answered.
"Share joy with others; don't take it away.
Why not give it a try?"

Determined to change, Bella waited for the park visitors to arrive.
Looking around, she decided to stop stealing their picnic lunches, and she made sure the ants stayed away so everyone could enjoy their food.

She uncovered the acorns so Sammy the
squirrel would have plenty to enjoy and
even enough to share.

Bella learned to catch the balloons, not pop them, and she always returned them as they flew away.
She sang with the sparrows and dropped crumbs for the ducks.
Bella stayed busy remembering to do something kind every day.

Agape Meadow Park was never the same.
Bella became one of the favorite
attractions in the park.
Everyone loved Bella. "Look, here comes
Bella!" The people would call out.
"She's my friend," the children shouted.
As it turned out, it wasn't long before
Bella began to love them too.

FRIEND OF THE PARK

The days passed, and one morning, Bella
awoke looking different.
Something remarkable had happened.
Bella's feathers started to change.
They became bright blue, purple, scarlet,
and utterly different from the other
blue jays.
The park animals called her Bella the
Beautiful.

"Oh! My... I wonder why this is happening," Bella asked.
Barry responded with his final answer. "You're not the same when real love touches you, Bella.
You become a new creation, and old things pass away. You become brand new. Always remember one thing, Bella: true love will change you and will change the world around you when you let it."

Bella gave Barry a big smile as she
watched him fly off.
"See you again, Bella," Barry cried out,
smiling back at her.
Off Barry flew, seeking his next
adventure. Where will it take him? What
will he find? Who will have ears to hear
his next message?
The End.

Epilogue:

The memory of Agape Meadow Park grew not just as a place of beauty, but as a place where love enters a heart and makes everything new.
A place where friendships grow and bring about change. A place where anything is possible, and miracles happen.

Conversation Starters:

1. Why do you think Bella acted like a bully in this story?

2. Did you ever have someone be unkind to you? How did it make you feel?

3. What helped Bella begin to change?

4. Do you think Bella's feathers changed when her heart changed?

5. Can you think of one kind thing you could do for someone today?

THE END!